About the Author

Mark Patterson was born in 1972 in Ashford, Kent. The 1970s were Mark's playground and as he grew up through the 1980s, he immersed himself in the popular culture of the era. Since then, Mark has never really lost sight of his formative years, and this interest in retro culture, combined with drawing skills and a sense of humour, provided the perfect cocktail for *Retroland*.

Mark Patterson

Retroland

A Humorous Look at 1970s & 1980s Britain

AUSTIN MACAULEY PUBLISHERS™
LONDON • CAMBRIDGE • NEW YORK • SHARJAH

Copyright © Mark Patterson (2018)

A CIP catalogue record for this title is available from the British Library.

First Edition Published: 2018 (Austin Macauley Publishers™ Ltd)

ISBN 9781528924320 (Paperback)
ISBN 9781528924337 (Hardback)
ISBN 9781528924344 (E-Book)

www.austinmacauley.com

This Edition Published (2018)
Austin Macauley Publishers™ Ltd.
25 Canada Square
Canary Wharf
London
E14 5LQ

Dedication

For Mum, Dad, Julie, Gavin, Ellie, Chloe and all my family and friends.

Thank you everyone who has supported and encouraged me, and to Seymour Harrison photographic shop in Folkestone, Kent.

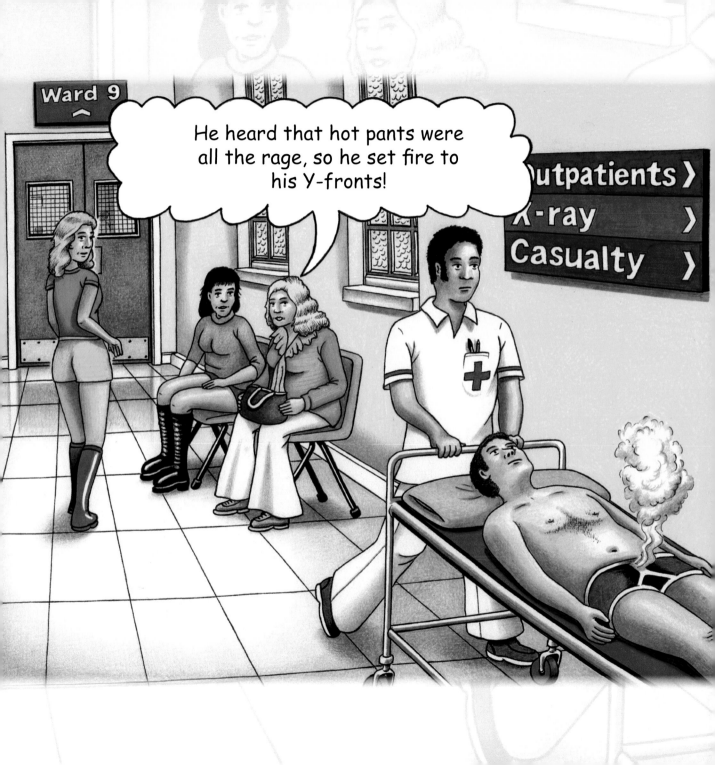

See David run.

Run David, run.

See Anne learn about antidisestablishmentarianism.

Learn about antidisestablishmentarianism Anne.

New word   About